MARGRET & H.A. REY'S
Curious George
Goes Camping

Illustrated in the style of H. A. Rey by Vipah Interactive

Houghton Mifflin Company   Boston 1999

Copyright © 1999 by Houghton Mifflin Company

Based on the character of Curious George®, created by Margret and H. A. Rey.
Illustrated by Vipah Interactive, Wellesley, Massachusetts: C. Becker, D. Fakkel, M. Jensen,
S. SanGiacomo, C. Yu.

The text of this book is set in 17-pt. Adobe Garamond.
The illustrations are watercolor and charcoal pencil, reproduced in full color.

Library of Congress Cataloging-in-Publication Data

Curious George goes camping / illustrated in the style of H. A. Rey by Vipah Interactive.
p. cm.
Based on the original character by Margret and H. A. Rey.
Summary: Curious George gets into mischief while camping but is able to redeem himself
in an emergency.
RNF ISBN 0-395-97831-9 PAP ISBN 0-395-97835-1 PABRD ISBN 0-395-97843-2
[1. Monkeys—Fiction. 2. Camping—Fiction.] I. Rey, Margret. II. Rey, H. A. (Hans
Augusto), 1898–1977. III. Vipah Interactive. IV. Title: Margret and H. A. Rey's Curious
George goes camping. V. Title: Curious George goes camping.
PZ7.M33585   1999
[E]—dc21   99-21453
                                            CIP

Manufactured in the United States of America

This is George.

He was a good little monkey, and always very curious.

This weekend George and his friend, the man with the yellow hat, had special plans. They were going camping!

At the campsite the man with the yellow hat unpacked their gear while George looked at all the tents. He saw tents for big families and

one just the right size for a puppy. There were even tents on wheels!

"Would you like to help me put up our tent, George?" the man asked.

George was happy to help. It would not
be hard to set up a tent, he thought.

But it wasn't easy!

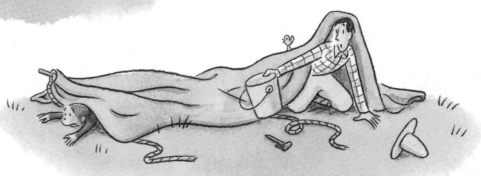

"George, why don't you fill our bucket with water at the pump?"
his friend suggested. "We'll need it by our campfire later, when we
roast marshmallows."

Mmm, marshmallows.
George loved marshmallows.
He couldn't wait to try them
roasted!

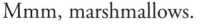

"Now don't wander off
and get into trouble," the
man warned. But George
did not hear him. He was
already gone.

At the pump George worked the handle up and down. Soon his bucket was full. On the way back down the trail, he saw a family packing up.

George watched a girl pour her bucket of water on a campfire.
The fire sizzled out.
George thought that looked like fun!

He poured his
bucket of water on
the next campfire.

"Hey," yelled a camper.
"We weren't finished with that yet!"
The camper began to chase George. But George didn't mean to cause
trouble. Now he only wanted to hide. He ran into the forest as fast as
he could, but the camper's footsteps followed close behind. George ran
faster and faster. The footsteps came closer and closer until, suddenly,

they were passing George. Why, it was not the camper chasing George now. It was a deer! What fun to run with a deer! Forgetting all about the camper and the marshmallows, George ran after the deer. But a little monkey cannot run as fast as a deer in the woods. Before long

George was lost and all alone. He felt tired and stopped to rest. At first he was worried—he was very far from camp. But there were lots

of other animals to keep him company. He saw a lizard sunning on a rock and a squirrel chattering in a tree. Then he saw the tail of a black

and white kitty peeking out from under a bush. He was curious. Would the kitty like to play? George gently pulled the kitty out...

PSSST!

But it was NOT a kitty!

It was a skunk—and it was scared. The skunk lifted its tail and sprayed.

WHEW! The spray smelled awful. The animals tried to get away. George wanted to get away, too. But he could not— the smell was all over him!

How would he ever get rid of
this awful smell? he wondered.

Too bad he could not take a bath
in the woods...

Then George had an idea. He could wash the smell off in the creek! George jumped into the cold water.

He splashed and scrubbed. But he was still smelly. And now he was wet, too.

But what could he do? George thought and thought. If he climbed up a tree to dry off, would the smell blow away?

No. Even dry and high up in the tree, George did not smell better. Poor George. He wished he hadn't wandered so far from camp. He wished he were roasting marshmallows with his friend. Suddenly George heard footsteps heading toward him. Someone was coming!

It was the
forest animals!
But they ran right
by him. They had seen
something scary. And George
saw it, too. It was a fire!

George had gotten into trouble for putting
out one fire, but this fire wasn't in the campground...

This was an emergency!
Quickly, George climbed
down the tree and grabbed
his bucket. He scooped it full
of water in the creek.

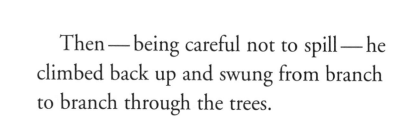

Then — being careful not to spill — he
climbed back up and swung from branch
to branch through the trees.

When George got close enough to the fire, he reached down and
poured the water on the flames. Out went the fire with a big hiss!
Just then George's friend rushed out of the forest with a ranger.

"George," he called, "I was afraid you would be here."

"It's a good thing you *were* here, George," the ranger said. "We saw smoke from the campground, but you put this fire out just in time."

George was glad to help. And the man with the yellow hat was glad to see that George was safe. But he had a funny look on his face.

"George," he asked, "what is that smell?"

Back at the campsite, George's friend helped him get rid of the awful smell. After a strange bath in tomato juice, George smelled fine.

Then the man with the yellow hat invited the ranger to cook dinner with them over their own small campfire.

"Fires can be nice, if you're careful," said the ranger.

George agreed.

Especially for roasting marshmallows.